Who Will Be My Valentine This Year?

Jerry Pallotta

David Biedrzycki

SCHOLASTIC INC.

New York   Toronto   London   Auckland
Sydney   Mexico City   New Delhi   Hong Kong

To my favorite valentines: Linda, Sheila, Jill, Mary, and Miriam!
— J.P.

To sweetheart librarians: Kathleen Smith, Ann Gargula, Ivey Carey, Bev Anderson,
Connie Patchett, Sue Pope, Sandy Kelly, Ann Rich, Joanna Schooley, Kim Gueldner,
Julie Goll, Jodi Vizzi, Danna Babione, Lisa Tucker, and Mary Pruitt
— D.B.

Text copyright © 2009 by Jerry Pallotta
Illustrations copyright © 2009 by David Biedrzycki
All rights reserved. Published by Scholastic Inc.
SCHOLASTIC and associated logos are trademarks
and/or registered trademarks of Scholastic Inc.
ISBN 978-0-545-23518-1

10 9 8 7 6 5 4 3 2 1   10 11 12 13 14

Printed in the U.S.A.   08
First printing this edition, December 2010

Tomorrow is February 14
and I'm looking for a valentine.

I have a pretty face and a beautiful smile.

I wonder who will be my valentine this year.

Leopard, will you be my valentine?

No way! I drive a car. You ride a bike.

Dolphin, will you be my valentine?

No! I wear a watch. You don't even know the time!

Butterfly, how about being valentines with me?

No, thank you! I read books. You like the movies.

Frog, will you be my valentine?

No! I use e-mail. You send postcards.

Elephant, please, please be my valentine!

No, I like chunky peanut butter! You like smooth.

Iguana, will you be my valentine?

I'm not interested! I like slides. You like swings.

Spider, we could be great valentines!

No, I wear sneakers. You always go barefoot!

Pigs, please, let's be valentines!

Burp! Bad idea. We eat like pigs. You have manners.

Turkey! Oh, Turkey! Will you be my valentine?

What's a valentine? I only know Thanksgiving.

Baboon, will you be valentines with me?

No! I like sunglasses. You like caps.

Lion, will you be —

ROAR! I won't even talk about it! *ROAR!*

Skunk, will you be my valentine?

No! I wear a tie. You never dress up.

Hippo, we were only kidding!

It's fun being different. We will *all* be your valentine!

Uh-oh! Now Rhinoceros is looking for a valentine!